PUFFIN BOOKS

WHEN MY NAUGHTY LITTLE SISTER WAS GOOD

Once upon a time, when my naughty little sister was just a little girl, she was visiting kind Mrs Cocoa Jones next door when she was washing all the lovely things from her china cupboard. There were plates with roses on, and teapots and vases and little Chinamen, and ladies with fans, and dishes, and my sister was so good that she didn't touch a thing.

Then Mrs Cocoa showed her a dear little china baby angel holding a white china basket with flowers in it.

'Oh, poor, poor angel,' said my sister. 'It hasn't got a head!' and she ran out of the house to her own little rockery and back again. 'Here it is, Mrs Cocoa. Here it is,' she said. 'Here's the baby angel's head. It was on my rockery,' and Mrs Cocoa told her what a good clever child she was to find the missing piece.

In fact, my naughty little sister seems to have become almost good in these stories about learning to talk, starting to sleep in a real bed, and mixing the Christmas puddings with her Granny, but she is just as lovable and funny as ever she was in her really naughty days in *My Naughty Little Sister*, *My Naughty Little Sister's Friends* and *My Naughty Little Sister and Bad Harry*.

When My Naughty Little Sister Was Good

DOROTHY EDWARDS

Illustrated by Shirley Hughes

PUFFIN BOOKS

Puffin Books, Penguin Books Ltd, Harmondsworth, Middlesex, England
Penguin Books, 625 Madison Avenue, New York, New York 10022, U.S.A.
Penguin Books Australia Ltd, Ringwood, Victoria, Australia
Penguin Books Canada Ltd, 2801 John Street, Markham, Ontario, Canada L3R 1B4
Penguin Books (N.Z.) Ltd, 182–190 Wairau Road, Auckland 10, New Zealand

—

Stories 1 to 7 first published by Methuen 1968
Stories 8, 9 and 10 published in *More Naughty Little Sister Stories*, Methuen, 1957
Published in Puffin Books 1973
Reprinted 1974 (twice), 1975, 1976, 1977, 1978, 1979, 1980, 1981

—

—

Set, printed and bound in Great Britain by
Cox & Wyman Ltd, Reading
Set in Monotype Bembo

Contents

FOR WINNIE WARNE WITH LOVE

I

My Naughty Little Sister
Learns to Talk

Once upon a time, when my sister and I were little
children, we had a very nice next-door neighbour called
Mrs Jones. Mrs Jones hadn't any children of her own,
but she was very fond of my sister and me.

Mrs Jones especially liked my sister. Even when she
was naughty! Even when she was a cross and noisy baby
with a screamy red face, Mrs Jones would be kind and
smily to her, and say, 'There's a ducky, then,' to her.

And sometimes Mrs Jones would be so kind and smily
that my bad little sister would forget to scream. She
would stare at Mrs Jones instead, and when Mrs Jones
said, 'Poor little thing, poor little thing,' to her, my
sister would go all mousy quiet for her. My naughty
little sister liked Mrs Jones.

When my sister was a very little baby girl, she
couldn't talk at all at first. She just made funny, blowy,
bubbly noises. But one day, without anyone telling her
to, she said, 'Mum, Mum,' to our mother.

We were surprised. We told her she was a very clever
baby. And because we were pleased she said, 'Mum,

Mum,' again. And again. She said it and said it and said it until we got very used to it indeed.

Then another day, when my sister was saying 'Mum, Mum,' and playing with her piggy toes, she saw our father looking at her, so she said, 'Dad, Dad,' instead!

Father was very excited, and so was Mother, because our funny baby was saying 'Mum, Mum,' and 'Dad, Dad,' as well. I was excited too, and so was dear Mrs Jones.

And because we were so excited my sister went on and on, saying 'Dad, Dad, Dad,' and 'Mum, Mum, Mum,' over and over again until Father, Mother and I weren't a bit excited any more. Only dear Mrs Jones went on being specially pleased about it. She *was* a nice lady!

So, one morning, when Mrs Jones looked over the fence and saw my baby sister in her pram, sucking her finger, she said, 'Don't suck your finger, ducky. Say "Dad, Dad," and "Mum, Mum," for Mrs Jones.'

And what do you think? My funny sister took her finger out of her mouth and said 'Doanes'. She said it very loudly, 'DOANES' – like that – and Mrs Jones was so astonished she dropped all her basket of wet washing.

'Doanes, Doanes, Doanes,' my sister said, because she couldn't quite say 'Jones', and Mrs Jones was so pleased, she left all her wet washing on the path, and ran in to fetch Mr Jones to come and hear.

Mr Jones who had been hammering nails in the

8

kitchen came out with a hammer in his hand and a nail in his mouth, running as fast as he could to hear my sister say 'Doanes'.

When she said it to him too, Mr Jones said my sister was a 'little knock-out', which meant she was very clever indeed.

After that my sister became their very special friend.

When she got bigger she started to say other words too, but Mr and Mrs Jones still liked it best when she said 'Doanes' to them. If she was in our garden and they were in their garden they always talked to her. Even when she could walk and get into mischief they *still* liked her.

One day a very funny thing happened. Mrs Jones was in her kitchen washing a lettuce for Mr Jones' dinner when she heard a little voice say 'Doanes' and there was my naughty little sister standing on Mrs Jones' back door-step. AND NO ONE WAS WITH HER.

And my little sister was smiling in a very pleased way.

The back gate was closed and the side gate was closed, and the fence was so high she *couldn't* have got over it.

Mrs Jones was very pleased to see my sister, and gave her a big, big kiss and a jam tart; but she was surprised as well, and said, 'How did you get here, ducky?'

But my little sister still didn't know enough words to tell about things. She just ate her jam tart, then she gave Mrs Jones a big kiss-with-jam-on, but she didn't say anything.

So Mrs Jones took my sister back to our house, and Mrs Jones and Mother wondered and wondered.

The very next day, when Mrs Jones was upstairs making her bed, she heard the little voice downstairs saying, 'Doanes, Doanes!', and there was my sister again!

And the back gate was shut, and the side gate was shut, and the fence was still too high for her to climb over.

Mrs Jones ran straight downstairs, and picked my sister up, and took her home again.

When Mr Jones came home, Mrs Jones told him, and Mother told Father, and they all stood in the gardens and talked. And my sister laughed but she didn't say anything.

Then I remembered something I'd found out when I

was only as big as my sister was then. Right up by a big bush at the back of our garden was a place in the fence where the wood wasn't nailed any more, and if you were little enough you could push the wood to the side and get through.

When I showed them the place, everybody laughed. My sister laughed very loud indeed, and then she went through the hole straight away to show how easy it was!

After that, my sister was always going in to see Mrs Jones, but because the hole was so small, and my sister was growing bigger all the time, Mr Jones found another place in his fence, and he made a little gate there.

It was a dear little white gate, with an easy up and down handle. There was a step up to it, and a step down from it. Mr Jones planted a pink rose to go over the top of it, and made a path from the gate to his garden path.

All for my sister. It was her very own gate.

And when Mrs Jones knocked on our wall at eleven o'clock every morning, and my sister went in to have a cup of cocoa with her, she didn't have to go through a hole in the fence, she went through her very own COCOA JONES' GATE.

2

My Naughty Little Sister's
Toys

Long ago, when my sister and I were little girls, we had a kind cousin called George who used to like making things with wood.

He made trays and boxes, and things with holes in to hang on the wall for pipes, and when he had made them he gave them away as presents.

George made me a chair for my Teddy-bear and a nice little bookcase for my story-books. Then George thought he would like to make something for my little sister.

Now that wasn't at all easy, because my sister was still a very little child. She still went out in a pram sometimes, she could walk a bit, but when she was in a great hurry she liked crawling better. She could say words though.

My sister had a very smart red pram. She liked her pram very much. She was always pleased when our mother took her out in it. She learned to say, 'pram, pram, pram,' when she saw it, and 'ride, ride, ride,' to show that she wanted to go out.

Well now, kind Cousin George was sorry to think that my sister liked crawling better than walking, so he said, 'I know, I will make her a little wooden horse-on-wheels so she can push herself along with it.'

And that is just what he did. He made a strong little wooden horse, with a long wavy tail, and a smily-tooth face that he painted himself. He painted the horse white with black spots. Then he put strong red wheels on it and a strong red handle. It was a lovely pushing-horse.

I said, 'Oh, isn't it lovely?' and I pushed it up and down to show my sister. 'Look, baby, gee-gee,' I said.

My sister laughed. She was so glad to have the wooden

horse. She stood up on her fat little legs and she got hold of the strong red handle, and she pushed too!

And when the horse ran away on his red wheels, my sister walked after him holding on to the red handle, and she walked, and WALKED. Clever Cousin George.

Mother said, 'That's a horse, dear. Say "Thank you, Cousin George, for the nice horse",' and she lifted my sister up so that she could give him a nice 'thank you' hug, because of course that was the way my sister thanked people in those days.

Then Mother said, 'Horse, horse, horse,' so that my sister could learn the new word, and she patted the wooden horse when she said it.

But my sister didn't say 'Horse' at all. *She* patted the wooden horse too, but she said, 'Pram, pram, pram.'

And she picked up her tiny Teddy-bear, and she laid him on the pushing-horse's back, and she picked up my doll's cot blanket and covered Teddy up with it, and she pushed the horse up and down, and said, 'Pram.'

When George came to see us again, he was surprised to find that my funny little sister had made the horse into a pram, but he said, 'Well, anyway, she can walk now!' And so she could. She had stopped crawling.

Because George liked my little sister he made her another nice thing. He made her a pretty little doll's house, just big enough for her to play with. It had a room upstairs, and a room downstairs, and there were some pretty little chairs and a table and a bed in it that he had made himself.

When my sister saw this doll's house she smiled and smiled. When she opened the front of the doll's house and saw the things inside she smiled a lot more.

She took all the chairs and things out of the doll's house and laid them on the floor, and she began to play with it at once. But she didn't play houses with it at all.

Because there was a room upstairs and a room downstairs and a front that opened she said it was an oven!

She pretended to light a light inside it, just as she had seen our mother do, when she was cooking the dinner, and she said, 'ov-en, ov-en.'

She called the chairs and table and the bed 'Dinner', and she put them back into the doll's house again, and

pretended they were cooking, while she took tiny Teddy for a ride on the pushing-horse pram.

She played and played with her doll's house oven and her pushing-horse pram.

Our Cousin George said, 'What an extraordinary child you are.' Then he laughed. 'That gives me an idea!' he said.

And when he went away he was smiling to himself.

The next time George came he was still smiling, and when my sister saw what he had made she smiled too. This time she knew what it was.

George had made a lovely wooden pretending-stove with two ovens and a pretending fire, and a real tin chimney. We don't have stoves like these nowadays, but some people still did when I was young. There was one in our Granny's house.

My sister said, 'Gran-gran oven,' at once.

I gave my little sister a toy saucepan and kettle from my toy box, and Mother gave her two little patty-tins.

George said, 'You can cook on the top, and in the ovens – just like Granny does.'

And that was just what my sister did do. She cooked pretending dinners on the wooden stove all day long, and Cousin George was very pleased to think she was playing in the right way with something he had made for her.

But that isn't the end of the story. Oh no.

One day my naughty little sister's bad friend Harry

came to visit us with his mother. He was only a little baby boy then, but he liked playing with my sister even in those days.

When my little sister saw Harry, she said, 'Boy-boy. Play oven.' She wanted Harry to cook dinners too.

Bad Harry looked at the wooden stove, and the real tin chimney and the pretending fire, and he said, 'Engine. Puff-puff.'

Then Harry pretended to put coal into the little fireplace. He opened the oven doors and banged them shut again just like the man who helped the engine-driver did, and he made choof-choof-choofy train noises.

Harry had been with his father to see the trains and he knew just the right noises to make and the right things to do.

My sister didn't know anything about trains then, but it was such a lovely game that she made all the noises Harry made and said 'Engine' too.

After that she and Harry had lots of lovely games playing engines with the little wooden stove.

When Cousin George heard about this, he said, 'Pram-horses and oven-doll's houses, and now – engine-stoves!'

He said, 'It's no good. When that child is a bigger girl I shall just give her some wood and some nails and let her make her own toys!'

I think he must have forgotten that he said this, because he never did give her any wood and nails. I wonder what she would have made if he had?

3

My Naughty Little Sister
and the Twins

When my sister was still quite a little child, she liked looking at herself in the looking-glass. She was always asking someone to lift her up so that she could see herself.

She would stare and stare at her funny little self. She made funny faces, and then she would laugh at the funny faces she had made, and then laugh all over again because the little girl in the glass was laughing. She used to amuse herself very much.

When my sister had first seen herself in the mirror she hadn't liked it at all. At first she had been pleased to see the small baby-girl, and had smiled, but when the baby in the glass smiled back, and she put out her hand to touch that baby-girl's smily face – there had only been cold, hard glass. It had been so nasty and so frightening that my poor little sister had cried and cried.

Mother hushed and hushed her and walked up and down with her, and said, 'Don't cry! Don't cry! It's only you, baby, it's you in the glass.'

When my sister stopped crying, my mother lifted

her up again, and said, 'It's you, baby, in the glass.'

And my sister looked at the poor teary baby in the glass, and she saw that the baby was copying her. She touched the glass again, and the baby touched it too. She got so interested she wasn't frightened any more. She said, 'Baby-in-the-glass!'

So after that, whenever my sister looked at herself in a looking-glass she said, 'Me. Me baby-in-glass.'

When she was neat and nice in a pretty new dress, she said, 'Smart baby-in-glass.' When she saw a dirty little face looking at her she said, 'Dirty baby-in-glass.'

She was a very funny child.

One day we went with our mother to fetch Father's shirts from the Washing Lady's house. Mother did most of our washing; but she sent Father's best shirts to the Washing Lady's house, because she washed them so beautifully and ironed them so cleverly they always looked like new.

Our Washing Lady had a funny little house. Inside her front door there was a room with pictures of ships on the wall, and photographs of sailors on the mantel-piece and seashells on the table.

The sailors were our Washing Lady's sons, and the ships were the ones they sailed the seas in. The Washing Lady was always talking about them.

There was always a steamy smell in the Washing Lady's house, because she was always boiling washing, and an ironing smell because she was always ironing things while the washing was boiling, and there was often a baking smell too, for this kind lady made beautiful curranty biscuits to give to the children who came with their mothers to fetch the washing.

My sister loved to go to the Washing Lady's house.

On the day I'm telling you about, a very funny thing happened when we got to the Washing Lady's house. We knocked at the door as we always did, and then we opened the door as we always did.

Out came a steamy smell and an ironing smell and a baking smell, just as they always did, too.

And then Mother called out, 'May I come in?'

And instead of the Washing Lady standing among the ship and sailor pictures and the seashells, we found two little tiny girls, standing hand in hand; and when they saw our mother and my little sister and me, they opened their mouths and they both called, 'Grandma, Grandma!'

My little sister stared and stared and stared. She looked at those little girls so much that they both stopped calling and stared back at her.

My sister stared so hard because those tiny little girls were absolutely alike. They had the same little tipping-up noses, the same little twinkly eyes, the same black, curly hair with red ribbons on, the same little blue dresses, the same red socks. *And they had both said 'Grandma' in the same little voices.*

Then the Washing Lady came out from the back room, and the two little alike girls ran to her, and hung on to her apron.

Mother said, 'These must be your Albert's twinnies then?'

And the Washing Lady said, 'Yes, they are.'

Albert was the Washing Lady's youngest sailor-son. She told Mother that the little girls had come to spend the day with her. She said, 'Albert's boat has come in and their Mother has gone to London to meet him.'

When she said this, the little looking-alike girls smiled again. They said, 'Our Daddy is coming home!'

One twinnie said, 'From over the sea – ' The other twinnie said, 'In a big, big boat – '

And the first twinnie said, 'And he's going to bring us – ' And the other one said, 'Lots and lots – '

And they both said together, 'Of lovely presents. HOORAY.'

And the funny twinnies fell right down on the floor and kicked their legs in the air to show how happy they were and they laughed and laughed.

My little sister thought they were so funny that she laughed and laughed too, and she fell on the floor and kicked *her* legs in the air. We all laughed then.

Then the Washing Lady told the twinnies to go and fetch the biscuit tin, and they went and fetched it. She gave me a curranty biscuit, and then one to my sister, then she gave one to each of the little twinnies. Then my little sister and the looking-alike girls sat down on the Washing Lady's front step to eat the biscuits, while their Grandma packed up Father's shirts.

When my sister finished eating her biscuit, she looked very hard at the twins. First at one twin, then at the other twin. Then she put out her hand and touched one little twinny face, and then the other twinny face. Then she touched her own face. She was very quiet, and then she said, 'Which is the looking-glass one?'

That silly little girl thought one twinnie was a real child, and one was a looking-glass child. That was why she touched their faces, and when she couldn't feel any cold, hard glass she was very, very puzzled.

'Which is the looking-glass baby?' she said.

'Good gracious me, what will you ask next?' said our mother. Then she remembered how my sister liked looking at herself in the glass. 'Why,' she said, 'she thinks only one of them is real!'

Our Washing Lady laughed, but she was a kind lady. She said, 'They are twinnies, dear. Two little girls. There are two looking-glass babies just like them.'

And although she was a very busy lady, she took my little sister and the twinnies upstairs to her bedroom, and showed my sister herself and *two* little looking-alike girls in the wardrobe mirror.

My sister looked at herself in the glass. She looked at the twinnies in the glass. Then she said, 'Thank you very much,' in a funny little voice.

And when we walked home she whispered to me, 'Is there another little real girl like me somewhere?'

I said, 'Oh no, there couldn't be anyone else like you – not anywhere.'

4

The Six Little Hollidays

Usually, when my sister and I were children, if our mother had to go anywhere special she would take my naughty little sister with her. But if it was somewhere very special indeed she left my sister with Mrs Cocoa Jones next door, or with Bad Harry's mother. Once my sister even spent a day at school with me.

But there was a time once, when Mrs Cocoa was away, and Bad Harry's mother was ill, when my mother didn't quite know what to do about getting my little sister minded.

Mother asked my teacher if my little sister could come to school again, but Teacher said that although she had been such a good child, she wouldn't be able to have her any more because she had minded some other little sisters in the school who hadn't been good at all. They had been so fidgety and naughty that she had had to say, no more minding!

The teacher said, 'I am afraid they are not all good like your little girl.'

Just fancy that!

Well, my mother was very anxious about my sister,

because she knew my sister could be very shy with people. She couldn't think of anyone who might want to mind a shy, cross girl for a whole afternoon.

When she was coming back from the school, she met a lady she knew and told her all about it. The lady was called Mrs Holliday, and Mrs Holliday said at once, 'Oh, don't worry about that. We will mind her with pleasure. We will call round for her at two o'clock.'

My mother was very glad that Mrs Holliday was going to mind my sister, although she couldn't help wondering if my sister would behave herself.

When our mother told my sister that she was going to spend an afternoon with Mrs Holliday my sister looked very cross and frightened. She stuck her lip out and her face went red as red, and our mother said, 'Oh dear, don't be awkward, will you?'

I think my sister *would* have been awkward. She might have bellowed and shouted, but just then there was a knock on our back door and there stood Mrs Holliday herself, all ready and smiling, and behind Mrs Holliday looking as shy and peeping as my little sister herself, were five little children: three little boys and two little girls.

Right up at the end of our garden by the back gate stood a very tall, very wide sort of perambulator-pushchair, and peeping out from under the hood of that was another little child!

My sister *did* stare, and all the little Hollidays stared. Mrs Holliday was a lady with red, rosy cheeks, and all the children had red, rosy cheeks too. And although they all wore different coloured coats and scarves they all wore bright blue woolly hats.

'We won't come in,' Mrs Holliday said, 'because our shoes are muddy.'

When my sister was ready, Mrs Holliday said, 'Come along, dear, don't take any notice of my children. They are all *very shy*, but they will talk nineteen to the dozen as soon as they are used to you.'

My sister was a shy child, but she had never seen so many shy children together before, and she quite forgot her own shyness when she saw them all hiding behind their mother.

Our mother said she hoped Mrs Holliday wouldn't find my sister too much for her, but Mrs Holliday said, 'One more will hardly be noticed.'

Then Mrs Holliday called the children out from behind her and said, 'These boys are John and David, and they are twins. This is Jean, and this is Susan, and they are twins too. The big boy is Tom, he has a bad arm, so he is not at school today, and the baby is Billy.'

Then Mrs Holliday told Jean and Susan to take my little sister's hands, and off they all went, all shy and quiet and peepy, down the garden to the back gate and the big perambulator-pushchair.

There sat baby Billy with his legs dangling down under a shiny black cover like a pram cover. He was peeping out from under a big black hood like a pram hood. There was a handle behind the hood like a push-chair handle.

My sister was so surprised to see this funny pram-pushchair, she said, 'That's a funny thing.'

When my sister said this, all the little Hollidays laughed together, and stopped being shy, because they thought it was a funny thing too, and then they waited for their mother to tell my little sister all about it.

Mrs Holliday said, 'It's a very special chair, this is. It was once used by FOREIGN ROYALTY.' And she looked so pleased and proud when she said this, that my sister knew it must be something very grand.

Mrs Holliday said, 'It was specially made for Royal Twins – that is why it is so wide; and although it's nearly fifty years old, it's still as good as new.'

Mrs Holliday said that as my sister was a visitor, she could ride with Billy in the royal pushchair, and my sister was so pleased she could hardly remember to say 'good-bye' to our mother.

Off they went down the street, Mrs Holliday behind the perambulator-pushchair with little Hollidays on either side, and my little sister very smiling and pleased and not shy, with Billy beside her. Billy was a dear little baby boy, and when he saw my sister was smiling and pleased, he was smiling and pleased too. They looked very happy children.

As they went along everybody they met smiled to see the funny pram-pushchair and the rosy Hollidays with their blue woolly hats and my happy little sister.

Mrs Holliday took them through the park, and they went a way my sister hadn't been before, so it was very interesting. In the park my sister got out of the pram-pushchair and ran and scuffled in the leaves with the other children. The leaves lay all over the paths, red and yellow and brown, and all the little Hollidays shouted with excitement and my sister shouted too.

When Mrs Holliday thought they had played enough they went off again. This time one of the little girl twins rode with Billy, and my little sister ran through the park with the other children. It was fun!

Outside the park, Tom, who had the bad arm, said, 'Before we go home we are going to the bakers, aren't we, Mother?'

And all the other little Hollidays shouted, 'Yes. Yes. For cookie-boys.'

They were all very excited, so my sister got excited too and they went down a street and stopped outside a funny little baker's shop.

Mrs Holliday said that as my sister hadn't been there before she could come in with her. All the Holliday children stood outside and pushed their faces against the window to watch.

Inside the shop was a dear old lady, and when she saw Mrs Holliday she said, 'I know what you have come for: six cookie-boys.'

But Mrs Holliday said, 'Not six. *Seven* today. I've got an extra little child, who has never had one of your cookie-boys before.'

The old lady said, 'Then I must find her a very nice one.'

She took down a big wooden tray, and in it there lay dozens and dozens of shiny brown cookie-boys.

Do you know what cookie-boys are? They are buns made in the shape of funny little men, with currant eyes and noses and mouths and rows of currants all down their fronts for buttons!

The old lady's cookie-boys were the shiniest and the stickiest cookie-boys ever made, and people came a long way to buy them.

The old lady put six cookie-boys in a bag for Mrs Holliday, and then she chose a special one and put it in a special bag for my little sister.

When they got to Mrs Holliday's house, they all sat round a big table and had tea and bread-and-butter and jam, and when they had eaten and eaten, they finished off with their cookie-boys.

My sister had just finished eating hers when our mother came to fetch her.

And what do you think? When she saw my mother, my sister began to cry and cry. She said, 'I don't want to go home yet.'

Our mother was very surprised.

But Mrs Holliday said, 'Now, be a good girl, and you shall come another day.'

And my sister stopped crying at once. And she did visit them again, too.

5

The Bonfire Pudding

When my sister was a little girl she didn't like Bonfire Night and fireworks. She didn't like them at all. I liked them very much and so did my sister's friend Harry, but she didn't.

She wouldn't even look out of the window on Bonfire Night.

She would say, 'It's burny and bangy, and I don't like it.'

So on Bonfire Nights, Mother stayed home with her, while our father took me out to let the fireworks off.

It was a pity because our mother *did* like fireworks.

Well now, one day, just before the Fifth of November (which is what Bonfire Night day is called) our mother took us round to our grandmother's house to pay a visit, and Mother told Granny all about my little sister not liking fireworks.

She said, 'It's such a pity, because this year the fireworks are going to be very grand. There is going to be a big bonfire on the common, and everyone is going there to let off fireworks.'

She said, 'There is going to be a Grand Opening with the Mayor, and a Band on a Lorry.'

Our mother said, 'I am sure she would like it. She likes music.'

But my sister looked very cross. She said, 'I do like music very much. But I don't like fireworks.'

Mother said, 'But they are going to have baked potatoes and sausages and spicy cakes and all sorts of nice things to eat.'

My sister said, 'I don't like bonfires.'

Mother said, 'You see, she is a stubborn child. She won't try to like them.'

But our Granny wasn't a bit surprised. She said, 'Well, I don't like bonfires or fireworks either. I never did. I was always glad to get my children out of the house on the Fifth of November. It gave me a chance to do something much more interesting.'

My little sister was glad to know that our grandmother didn't like fireworks either, so she went right up to Granny's chair and held her hand.

Granny said, 'You don't like fireworks and no more do I. Why don't you come and visit me on Firework Night? I think I can find something interesting for you to do.'

When Granny said this, she shut one of her eyes up, and made a funny face at my sister. She said, 'Why don't you come and have some fun with me? Then your

mother can go to the common with your daddy and sister and have fun too.'

My sister made a funny face back at Granny, and said, 'Yes, I think I should like that.'

So on Bonfire Night, before it got too dark, Mother wrapped my little sister up in a warm coat and a big shawl and put her in a pushchair and hurried round to Grandmother's house.

She left my sister as soon as Granny opened the door, because she was in a hurry to get back.

'Come in,' said Granny to my little sister. 'You are just in time.' She helped my sister take her things off, and then she said, 'Now, into the kitchen, Missy.'

It was lovely and warm in the kitchen in our Granny's house. My sister was very pleased to see the big fire and the black pussy asleep in front of it.

'Look,' said Granny. 'It's all ready.'

Granny's big kitchen table looked just like a shop, there were so many things on it. There were jars and bottles and packets, full of currants and sultanas and raisins and ginger and candied peel, and a big heap of suet on a board, and a big heap of brown sugar on a plate. There were apples and oranges and lemons and, even some big clean carrots!

There was a big brown bowl standing on a chair that had a big, big, wooden spoon in it. And on the draining board were lots of white basins.

Can you guess? My sister couldn't. She didn't know

what all this stuff was for, so Granny said, 'We are going to make the Family Christmas Puddings. I always make one for every one of my children every year. And I always make them on Bonfire Night. IT TAKES MY MIND OFF THE BANGS.'

My sister was very surprised to hear this, and to know that all these lovely things to eat were going to be made into Christmas Puddings.

Granny said, 'You can help me, and it will take your mind off the bangs, too.'

She said, 'I've looked out a little apron; it will just fit you. It used to belong to one of your aunties when she was a little girl.'

And she tied a nice white apron round my sister's little middle.

'Now,' Granny said, 'climb up to the sink, and wash and scrub your hands. They must be clean for cookery.'

So my sister climbed up to the sink and washed her hands, and Granny dried them for her, and then she was ready to help.

Granny found lots of things for her to do, and they laughed all the time.

Granny was quick as quick, and every time my sister finished doing one thing, she found something else for her to do at once.

Granny poured all the currants out on to the table and my sister looked to see if there were any stalky bits left in them. When she had done that, Granny told her to

take the almonds out of the water, and pop them out of their brown skins. That was a lovely thing to do. When my sister popped an almond into her mouth Granny only laughed and said, 'I'll have one as well.'

Granny chopped the suet, then the almonds, and the ginger while my sister put the currants and sultanas and things into the big brown bowl for her. It was quite a hard job because she had to climb up and down so much, but she did it, and she didn't spill anything either. Granny was pleased.

Grandmother chopped the candied peel, and because my sister was so good and helpful she gave her one of the lovely, sugary, candied peel middles to suck.

While Granny crumbled bread and chopped apples and carrots, she let my sister press the oranges and lemons in the squeezer.

All the time they chattered and laughed and never thought about Bonfire Night. They never noticed the bangs.

Once the black pussy jumped out of the chair and ran and hid himself under the dresser, but they were laughing so much they didn't even notice.

At the very end, Granny broke a lot of eggs into a basin; then she held the mixer while my sister turned the handle to beat them up.

And sometimes, while they were working, Granny would make a funny face at my sister, and eat a sultana, and sometimes my sister would make a funny face at Granny and eat a raisin!

When all the things had been put into the brown bowl, Granny began to mix and mix with the big spoon. She gave my sister a little wooden spoon so that she could mix too.

Then, Granny said, 'Now you must shut your eyes and stir, and make a wish. You always wish on a Christmas pudding mixture.'

And my sister did. She shut her eyes and turned her spoon round and round. Then Granny shut her eyes and wished.

My sister said, 'I wished I could come and help you next Bonfire Night, Granny.'

And Granny said, 'Well, Missy, that was just what I wished too!'

Then my sister sat quietly by the fire while our grandmother put the pudding mixture into all the basins, and covered them with paper and tied them with cloth.

My sister was very tired now, but she sat smiling and watching until Father came to fetch her.

Our father said, 'Goodness, Mother, do you still make the Christmas Puddings on Bonfire Night? Why, you used to when I was a boy.'

Granny said, 'This little girl and I think Bonfire Night is the best time of all for making Christmas puddings.'

She said, 'You may as well take your pudding now. It must be boiled all day tomorrow and again on

Christmas Day. It should be extra good this year, as I had such a fine helper!'

So Father brought it home that night and on Christmas Day we had it for dinner.

My sister was so proud when she saw it going into the water on Christmas morning she almost forgot her new toys.

And when we were sitting round the table, and Father poured brandy on it, and lit it, so that the pudding was covered with little blue flames, my sister said, 'Now it's a real bonfire pudding.'

6

Harry's Shouting Coat

Long ago, when my sister was a funny little girl with a friend called Harry, Harry had an auntie who lived over the sea in Canada, and this auntie used to send Harry presents.

Sometimes she sent him toys, sometimes she sent him sweeties. But once she sent him a very bright coat.

It was the loveliest coat Harry had ever seen. It was the loveliest coat my little sister had ever seen.

It was bright, bright red, and it had a bright, bright yellow collar and bright, bright yellow pockets and shiny goldy buttons and there was white twisty cord round the buttons.

My sister was playing at Harry's house when the coat-parcel came, and they were both very excited.

Harry tried the coat on at once, and walked up and down to show my sister, and then my sister tried it on and walked up and down to show Harry.

But do you know, Harry's mother didn't like that coat at all! She said, 'I really don't think you can wear it to go out in. It's far too loud.'

49

When she showed the coat to Harry's father, he said, 'Yes, it's loud all right. It shouts.'

Harry's father and mother laughed then. But Harry didn't laugh and my sister didn't laugh. Harry was thoroughly cross. He said, 'It's a very nice coat. Auntie sent it for me. I want to wear it.'

His father said, 'Well, you can wear it in the garden and frighten the birds with it. Then they won't eat all the seeds.'

But Harry didn't want to wear that beautiful coat in the garden. He wanted to wear it where all the other children could see it. My sister wanted him to wear it where all the other children could see it too. She wanted to be with him when everyone was looking at his smart red coat.

She said, 'I think it's a beautiful coat, Harry.'

Harry said, 'I want to wear it outside.' Harry was very cross when he said, 'I want to wear it,' but he didn't shout. He had a little, little cross voice.

Harry had a shouting voice too. He used to shout at my naughty little sister sometimes, but he had a little, cross voice too.

Harry's mother didn't like to be unkind about the red coat because after all it was Harry's present, so she had a good idea. She said, 'All right, you can wear it out one day if you are a *very good boy*.'

She said this because she thought Harry wouldn't be good.

But he was.

Those two naughty children went out into the garden, and whispered and whispered and they made up their minds that Harry would be good, and he was!

My sister helped him to be good. She didn't quarrel with him or grumble at him. She was good and polite to him, and Harry was good and polite to her. Do you know how they managed it? They played a game of being good and polite people. It was fun!

When Harry was at home he was still good. He helped his father and tidied up his toys, and he kept saying to his mother, 'Haven't I been good enough yet?' Until at last she said Harry could wear his coat tomorrow.

She said she would take Harry and my sister for a picnic on the Island and Harry could wear his red coat.

Harry and my sister were very pleased about this, because they liked going to the Island very much.

The Island was in the middle of the river. There was an old man in a sailor hat and a blue coat to row you in a boat to the Island, and to come and fetch you later on. He was the ferryman.

It was lovely to sit in the boat with the water all round you. You had to sit very still on the seats or the old man shouted at you. So you couldn't play anything, but it was still very nice.

Sometimes there were lots of people going to the Island, but on this picnic day when Harry wore his loud red coat, there was only Harry's mother, and Harry and my little sister.

The old ferryman wasn't there either. There was just a boy to row the boat. The boy said the old man was his Grandad. He said his Grandad had gone to get some new teeth, but he would be back later on.

Harry and my sister were disappointed there were no

other people going to the Island; they wanted to show off the coat. Lots of people had stared when they went through the town, and they had been very proud. A postman had said, 'My, my!' and a boy had whistled, and some people had come out of a shop to look. It had been exciting.

Harry's mother said she wasn't sorry no one else was going to the Island.

Although there were no other people, Harry and my sister had a lovely time. They ran all round the Island first. Then they played house-on-fire. My sister sat under a bush that was the house, and Harry was the fire-engine and the fireman too in his red coat and shiny buttons.

Then they ate their picnic, and Harry's mother said she would have a little nap before the ferryman came to fetch them. Harry said he would have a nap too, because he had got hot and tired running about in his coat all the time and my sister said she would have a nap as well as there wouldn't be anyone to play with, so she lay down too, and soon everyone was fast asleep!

Harry's mother woke up first of all, and when she woke up she was very worried. She woke Harry and my sister up, and they were very cross and sleepy at first.

She said, 'Oh, do wake up properly, children. It's late and the boat hasn't come.'

They all ran to look across the river then, and Harry and my sister forgot to be sleepy because Harry's mother was so worried.

They saw the boat tied up across the river, but there was no boat boy and no old ferryman.

Harry's mother said, 'Oh dear, they have forgotten us!'

When she said this, my sister started to cry, because it sounded so nasty to be forgotten, and then Harry cried too, and his mother had to make a fuss of them until they stopped.

'Never mind,' she said. 'We will wait, and when we see anyone we will call out, and they will know we are here.'

They waited and waited, and, just as they were beginning to think they might have to sleep on the Island all night, they saw the old man in his sailor hat coming down the path by the boat.

They shouted and shouted. But the old man took no notice. They shouted again, but he didn't hear them.

He looked across. He stood still, then he waved and waved to them. He untied the boat, got in it, and began to row and row, straight to the Island.

They were glad to see him.

When he rowed them back, he told Harry's mother that his grandson had forgotten to tell him about them. He said, 'I was just coming to put the boat away.'

Harry's mother said, 'It's a good thing we shouted, then.'

But the old man said, 'I didn't hear any shouting, Mam. I didn't hear anything.'

He said, 'If I hadn't looked across and seen this young chap's coat, I shouldn't have known anyone was here.'

When the old man said this, Harry looked at my little sister and she looked at him. 'Father said the coat shouted,' Harry said.

'It's a good thing it was *loud*,' said my sister. 'I don't think I would like to sleep on the Island very much.'

When they got home again, Harry's mother said, 'Well, at least you won't get lost in that coat. It's too conspicuous. I think you had better wear it when we go to the park or one of the other places you sometimes get lost in.'

And that is just what Harry did. Sometimes, when they played in the park, he let my sister borrow it for a treat, so that she could run about in the bracken without getting lost.

7

The Baby Angel

When I was a little girl, and my sister was a little girl, our dear next-door friend Mrs Cocoa Jones was always washing and dusting and polishing her clean, tidy house.

My little sister often went to visit Mrs Jones when she was doing her work. Sometimes she helped her, and sometimes she just sat and watched.

Mr Cocoa Jones was always busy too. He painted and sawed and nailed and glued things. He stuck up wallpaper and mended pipes. When he wasn't doing these things he would go outside and do something new to his garden.

He didn't just plant flowers and vegetables like our father. Oh no! He made pretty paths with big stones, and stuck sea-shells like fans all along the edges. He put a big stone basin on top of a pipe for the birds to bath in, and he made a garden seat for Mrs Cocoa out of twisty branches. My sister used to love watching clever Mr Jones at work.

One day Mr Jones brought home a big barrowful of rocks and stones. He put all these stones in a heap by his

back door. Then he put lots of earth on the heap, and
planted flowers in the earth.

My sister said, 'What are you doing that for, Mr
Cocoa?' and Mr Cocoa said he was making a rockery.
He said in the summer, when the flowers were out, it
would make a nice bit of colour.

And when the summer came Mr Cocoa's rockery was
very beautiful. It was so beautiful that Mother said she
would like a rockery too, and Father said he would
make one for her next spring.

My sister said she would like a rockery as well, but
she didn't wait at all. She went down to the rubbishy
end of our garden, and collected lots of bricks and stones
and earth and made herself a little rockery right away.

My funny sister made her rockery, but she didn't put flowers on it like Mr Cocoa did. She looked all over our rubbish heap and found pieces of blue glass and red glass and broken china with pretty patterns on it, and she stuck them on her rockery instead.

Mr Cocoa said my sister's rockery was a good idea, because it would be pretty all the year round. He said his rockery was only pretty when the flowers were out.

My little sister smiled a lot then, and kind Mr Cocoa said if she wanted any more things for her rockery she could come and look at his rubbish heap, and see if she could find anything. 'Only mind you don't cut yourself on something sharp,' Mr Cocoa said, 'or I'll have Mrs Jones after me!'

My sister found a lot of interesting things for her rockery on the Cocoa Jones' rubbish heap. She found pieces of china and glass, and a piece of an old bubble-pipe. She found one of those diamond-looking, sparkly bottle stoppers, and one of Mr Cocoa's path shells that he had thrown away because he didn't need it. She found half a little crockery dog, and a *round white china thing*, with a pretty little china face on it.

My sister was very pleased with all these things, and she put them on her rockery as well. She put the little half-dog on the top, and the pretty smiling-face thing in front where it smiled and smiled. Everybody said her rockery looked very pretty. Even Father, and he didn't often say things like that.

Well now, one day when my sister went to visit Mrs Cocoa, she found that dear lady very busy. Mrs Cocoa had a very beautiful best front-room, and in this room was a big glass cupboard with all Mrs Cocoa's very best china in it.

When my sister came in, Mrs Cocoa was washing all her lovely china from the glass cupboard, and she said, if my sister would promise not to touch anything, she could come and stand on the stool by the table and watch her.

Mrs Jones had lots of lovely china, and she washed it all very carefully in soapy water, and dried it very, very carefully on an old soft towel. She had plates with roses on, and teapots and vases and little Chinamen, and ladies with fans, and dishes, and tiny red drinking glasses. My sister hadn't seen all these things close to before, but she only looked; she didn't touch a thing!

When Mrs Cocoa was washing a black teapot with yellow daisies on it, she said, 'Oh dear! There's something in here!'

My sister looked to see what was in the teapot, and Mrs Jones showed her a wet, soapy paper bundle.

'Oh dear,' said Mrs Cocoa. 'I'd forgotten about the baby angel.'

And she carefully opened the wet soapy paper, and inside was a white china baby angel with tiny wings and no clothes on. It was holding a white china basket with white flowers in it.

My sister looked hard at the little angel. She said, 'Oh, poor, poor angel. It hasn't got a head!' And it hadn't.

Mrs Cocoa said, 'All this china came from my old auntie's. The little angel was broken when we unpacked it, but Mr Jones said he would mend it for me.'

Then she told my sister that Mr Cocoa hadn't been able to mend it because the head had disappeared.

Mrs Cocoa said, 'I suppose it must have got burned up when Mr Jones got rid of all the paper the china was wrapped in. It's such a shame. I always loved that little angel when I was a girl!'

My sister looked hard at that baby angel, and then she remembered something. She remembered the round china white thing with the pretty smiling face that she had put on her rockery.

She didn't say a word to Mrs Cocoa. She slipped off the stool, and ran out of the house, through her own little gate, up our garden, straight to her rockery and back again.

'Here it is, Mrs Cocoa. Here it is,' my sister said. 'Here's the baby angel's head. It was on my rockery.'

Mrs Cocoa Jones was delighted. She ran in to tell Mother about my sister's cleverness in finding the baby angel's little head. She told Mr Jones when he came home, and he got out his sticky glue and stuck it on at once. It looked very pretty when it was mended.

Mrs Cocoa took the baby angel in to show my sister,

and my sister saw that it was smiling at the basket of white flowers.

'You are a good, clever child!' Mrs Cocoa said. She said that if my sister hadn't been so clever and made such a lovely rockery she would never have found the angel's head. She said it must have fallen out of the paper when Mr Cocoa burned the rubbish many years ago.

Mrs Cocoa said, 'I prize that little angel very much.' But she said that when my sister was a lady of twenty-one she would give her the baby angel for her very own! Wasn't that kind of her?

She did too, and if you go to my good, grown-up sister's house you will see the baby angel smiling at his flowers on my sister's mantelpiece.

8

My Naughty Little Sister
Shows Off

Do you like climbing? My naughty little sister used to like climbing very much indeed. She climbed up fences and on chairs and down ditches and round railings, and my mother used to say, 'One day that child will fall and hurt herself.'

But our father said, 'She will be all right if she is careful.'

And my little sister *was* careful. She didn't want to hurt herself. She climbed on *easy things*, and when she knew she had gone far enough, she always came down again, slowly, slowly, carefully, carefully – one foot down – the other foot down – like that.

My little sister was so careful about climbing that our father nailed a piece of wood on to our front gate, so that she would have something to stand on when she wanted to look over it. There was a tree by the gate, and Father put an iron handle on the tree to help her to hold on tight. Wasn't he a kind daddy?

Well now, one day my naughty little sister went

down to the front gate because she thought it would be nice to see all the people going by.

She climbed up carefully, carefully, like a good girl, and she held on to the iron handle, and she watched all the people going down the street.

First the postman came along. He said, 'Hello, Monkey,' and that made her laugh. She said, 'Hello, postman, have you any letters for this house?' and the postman said, 'Not today I'm afraid, Monkey.'

My little sister laughed again because the postman called her 'Monkey', but she remembered to hold on tight.

Then Mr Cocoa Jones went by on his bicycle. Mr Cocoa said, 'Don't fall,' and he ling-a-linged his bicycle bell at her. 'Be very careful,' said Mr Cocoa Jones, and 'ling-a-ling', said Mr Cocoa Jones' bell.

My naughty little sister said, 'I won't fall. I won't fall, Mr Cocoa. I'm sensible,' and Mr Cocoa ling-a-linged his bell again and called 'Good-bye'.

My naughty little sister waved to Mr Cocoa. She waved very carefully. She didn't lean forward to see him go round the corner or anything silly like that. No, she was most careful.

She was careful when the nice baker came with the bread. She climbed down, carefully, carefully and let him in.

She was careful when cars went by. She held tight and stood very still. She saw a steam-roller and a rag-a'-bone man, and she held very tight indeed.

Then my naughty little sister saw her friend, Bad Harry, coming down the road, and she forgot to be sensible. She began to show off.

My little sister shouted, 'Harry, Harry look at me. I'm on the gate, Harry.'

Bad Harry did look at her, because she called in such a loud voice, 'Look at me!' like that.

Then my silly little sister stood on one leg only – just because she wanted Bad Harry to think that she was a clever girl.

That made Bad Harry laugh, so my little sister showed

off again. She stood on the other leg only, and then – *she let go of the tree and waved her arms.*

And then – she fell right off the gate. Bump! She fell down and bumped her head.

Oh dear! Her head *did* hurt, and my poor little sister cried and cried. Bad Harry cried too, and my mother came hurrying out of the house to see what had happened.

Our dear mother said, 'Don't cry, don't cry, baby,' in a kind, kind voice. 'Don't cry, baby dear,' she said, and she picked my little sister up and took her indoors and Bad Harry followed them. They were still crying and crying.

They cried so much that my mother gave them each a sugar lump to suck. Then they stopped crying because they found that they couldn't cry and suck at the same time.

Then our mother looked at my little sister's poor head. 'What a nasty bruise,' our mother said. 'I think I had better put something on it for you, and you must be a good brave girl while I do it.'

My little sister was a good brave girl, too. She held Bad Harry's hand very tight, and she shut her eyes while Mother put some stingy stuff out of a bottle on to her poor head. Our mother did it very quickly, and my brave sister didn't fidget and she didn't cry. Wasn't she good?

When our mother had finished she gave my little

sister and her friend, Bad Harry, an apple each and they
went into the garden to play.

They had a lovely time playing in the garden. First
they picked dandelions and put them in the water-tub
for boats. Then they played hide-and-seek among the
cabbages. Then they made a little house underneath the
apple-tree. Then they found some blue chalk and drew
funny old men on the tool-shed door.

And my little sister forgot all about her poor head.

When our father came home and saw my naughty
little sister playing in the garden he said, 'Hello, old
lady, have you been in the wars?' and my little sister
was surprised because she had forgotten all about falling

off the gate. Father said, 'You have got a nasty lump on top!'

So my little sister thought she would go indoors and look at her nasty lump. She climbed up on to a chair to look at herself in the mirror on the kitchen wall, and she saw that there was a big bump on her forehead. It was all yellowy-greeny.

Our mother said, 'Climbing again! I should think you would have had enough climbing for one day!'

My little sister looked at her big bump in the mirror, and then she climbed down from the chair, carefully, carefully.

She climbed down very carefully indeed, and do you know what she said? She said, 'I like climbing very much, but I don't like falling down. And I *certainly* don't like nasty bumps on my head. So I don't think I will be a showing off girl any more.'

9

My Naughty Little Sister and the Baby

One day, long ago, when I was a little girl and my naughty little sister was a very little girl, a lady called Mrs Rogers asked my mother if she would mind her little boy-baby for the afternoon.

My mother was very pleased to help Mrs Rogers. 'I should be glad to mind the baby,' she said.

I was very pleased to think we were going to have a little boy-baby in our house for a whole afternoon, but my little sister said, 'I don't know babies, do I?'

Our mother said, 'No, but I expect you will know this one quite well by the time Mrs Rogers comes for it. You can't help knowing babies,' our mother said.

And my little sister said, 'Well, I hope I am glad when I know it.'

Well now, when Mrs Rogers came, my silly sister would not go out to look at the baby, she stood at the door and behaved in a very shy and peepy way and waited for our mother to call her.

'Come and look at the boy-baby,' said Mother, and she took my sister by the hand to look at the baby in the pram.

He was a very dear baby. He was kicking and cooing and smiling and looking very happy.

'Isn't he nice?' my mother said.

My little sister didn't say, 'Yes, he is nice' because she didn't know the baby very well then, she said, 'He's very fat.'

My mother told my little sister, 'All babies are fat. *You* were fat too,' she said.

My little sister was very surprised to hear that she had been fat like the boy-baby. She stuck out her tummy and blew out her cheeks to look fat, and said, 'Fat girl.'

When the baby saw my little sister pretending to be fat, he began to laugh, and when he laughed he showed a little white tooth. 'Look, a toothy,' said my little sister, and when she said 'Look, a toothy', that little boy-baby laughed very loudly indeed, and he took off his white woolly cap and he threw it right out of the pram!

My little sister picked up the white woolly cap for the baby.

'Put it back on his head,' our mother said, and my little sister did put it back on his head, and do you know, the bad boy-baby pulled his cap straight off again and threw it out of the pram!

So – my little sister picked the cap up *again* – and put it on the boy-baby's head *again*, and that naughty boy pulled it off and threw it away and laughed and laughed, and my little sister laughed as well because the boy-baby was so jolly and so fat.

Then my little sister talked to the baby. 'You must keep your cap *on*,' she said, and she pulled it on very carefully and tightly, and when he tried to pull it off again it only fell over one of his eyes.

Then my little sister put his cap straight, and *then* she did a very clever thing to make him forget all about his cap. She popped her old doll, Rosy-primrose, round the side of the pram, and said, 'Boh.' And the boy-baby was so pleased he giggled and giggled.

So my little sister popped Rosy-primrose round the pram again and again, and each time the funny baby giggled and my little sister giggled. Mother laughed and I laughed too to see my funny sister and the funny boy-baby.

Then my little sister said to the boy-baby, 'What is your name?' and the boy-baby laughed again and said, 'Ay-ay.'

'Where do you live?' asked my little sister, and the boy-baby said 'Ay-ay' again. Then the baby said, 'Oigle, oigle, oigle,' and my sister said, 'That's a funny thing to say.'

My mother said, 'He doesn't talk properly yet. *You* didn't talk when you were a baby.'

What a surprise for my naughty little sister. 'Not talk!'

When tea-time came the baby sat in the old high-chair next to my naughty little sister, and my mother gave him some crusts with butter on them.

That bad baby dropped some of his crusts on the floor, and sucked some of them, and waved some of them about, and then he tried to push a crust into my little sister's ear. She was cross!

But our mother told her that the baby was too little to know any better, so my little sister forgave the baby and laughed at him.

When tea was over, the baby lay in his pram and played with his toes, and then he fell asleep. He was fast asleep when Mrs Rogers came to take him home.

When my naughty little sister went to bed that night, do you know what she did? She pretended that she couldn't talk, she said, 'Ay-ay, ay-ay,' and played with her toes just like the boy-baby did.

Then she *did* speak, she said, 'I know lots about babies now, don't I?'

My Naughty Little Sister
and the Big Girl's Bed

A long time ago, when my naughty little sister was a very small girl, she had a nice cot with pull-up sides so that she couldn't fall out and bump herself.

My little sister's cot was a very pretty one. It was pink, and had pictures of fairies and bunny-rabbits painted on it.

It had been my old cot when I was a very small child and I had taken care of the pretty pictures. I used to kiss the fairies 'good night' when I went to bed, but my bad little sister did not kiss them and take care of their pictures. Oh no!

My naughty little sister did dreadful things to those poor fairies. She scribbled on them with pencils and scratched them with tin-lids, and knocked them with poor old Rosy-primrose her doll, until there were hardly any pictures left at all. She said, 'Nasty fairies. Silly old rabbits.'

There! Wasn't she a bad child? You wouldn't do things like that, would you?

And my little sister jumped and jumped on her cot.

After she had been tucked up at night-time she would get out from under the covers, and jump and jump. And when she woke up in the morning she jumped and jumped again, until one day, when she was jumping, the bottom fell right out of the cot, and my naughty little sister, and the mattress, and the covers, and poor Rosy-primrose all fell out on to the floor!

Then our mother said, 'That child must have a bed!' Even though our father managed to mend the cot, our mother said, 'She must have a bed!'

My naughty little sister said, 'A big bed for me?'

And our mother said, 'I am afraid so, you bad child. You are too rough now for your poor old cot.'

My little sister wasn't ashamed of being too rough for her cot. She was pleased because she was going to have the new bed, and she said, 'A big girl's bed for me!'

My little sister told everybody that she was going to have a big girl's bed. She told her kind friend the window-cleaner man, and the coalman, and the milkman. She told the dustman too. She said, 'You can have my old cot soon, dustman, because I am going to have a big girl's bed.' And she was as pleased as pleased.

But our mother wasn't pleased at all. She was rather worried. You see, our mother was afraid that my naughty little sister would jump and jump on her new bed, and scratch it, and treat it badly. My naughty little sister had done such dreadful things to her old cot, that my mother was afraid she would spoil the new bed too.

Well now, my little sister told the lady who lived next door all about her new bed. The lady who lived next door to us was called Mrs Jones, but my little sister used to call her Mrs Cocoa Jones because she used to go in and have a cup of cocoa with her every morning.

Mrs Cocoa Jones was a very kind lady, and when she heard about the new bed she said, 'I have a little yellow eiderdown and a yellow counterpane upstairs, and they are too small for any of my beds, so when your new bed comes, I will give them to you.'

My little sister was excited, but when she told our mother what Mrs Cocoa had said, our mother shook her head.

'Oh dear,' she said, 'what will happen to the lovely eiderdown and counterpane when our bad little girl has them?'

Then, a kind aunt who lived near us said, 'I have a dear little green nightie-case put away in a drawer. It belonged to me when I was a little girl. When your new bed comes you can have it to put your nighties in like a big girl.'

My little sister said, 'Good. Good,' because of all the nice things she was going to have for her bed. But our mother was more worried than ever. She said, 'Oh dear! That pretty nightie-case. You'll spoil it, I know you will!'

But my little sister went on being pleased as pleased about it.

Then one day the new bed arrived. It was a lovely shiny brown bed, new as new, with a lovely blue stripy mattress to go on it: new as new. And there was a new stripy pillow too. Just like a real big girl would have.

My little sister watched while my mother took the poor old cot to pieces, and stood it up against the wall. She watched when the new bed was put up, and the new mattress was laid on top of it. She watched the new pillow being put into a clean white case, and when our mother made the bed with clean new sheets and clean new blankets, she said, 'Really big-girl! A big girl's bed – all for me.'

Then Mrs Cocoa Jones came in, and she was carrying the pretty yellow eiderdown and the yellow counterpane. They were very shiny and satiny like buttercup flowers, and when our mother put them on top of the new bed, they looked beautiful.

Then our kind aunt came down the road, and *she* was carrying a little parcel, and in the little parcel was the pretty green nightie-case. My little sister ran down the road to meet her because she was so excited. She was more excited still when our aunt picked up her little nightdress and put it into the pretty green case and laid the green case on the yellow shiny eiderdown.

My little sister was so pleased that she was glad when bedtime came.

And, what do you think? She got carefully, carefully into bed with Rosy-primrose, and she laid herself down and stretched herself out – carefully, carefully like a good, nice girl.

And she didn't jump and jump, and she didn't scratch the shiny brown wood, or scribble with pencils or scrape with tin-lids. Not ever! Not even when she had had the new bed a long, long time.

My little sister took great care of her big girl's bed. She took great care of her shiny yellow eiderdown and counterpane and her pretty green nightie-case.

And whatever do you think she said to me?

She said, 'You had the fairy pink cot before I did. But this is my very own big girl's bed, and I am going to take great care of my very own bed, like a big girl!'

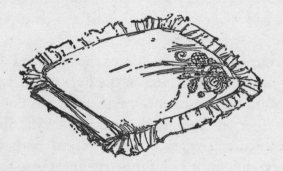